The Odyssey

Jan Pieńkowski & David Walser

For Judith

PUFFIN BOOKS

UK | USA | Canada | Ireland | Australia | India | New Zealand | South Africa

Puffin Books is part of the Penguin Random House group of companies whose addresses can be found at global.penguinrandomhouse.com.

www.penguin.co.uk   www.puffin.co.uk   www.ladybird.co.uk

Penguin
Random House
UK

First published 2019

001

Text copyright © David Walser, 2019

Illustrations copyright © Jan Pieńkowski, 2019

The moral right of the author and illustrator has been asserted

Made and printed in China

A CIP catalogue record for this book is available from the British Library

ISBN: 978–0–241–29879–4

All correspondence to: Puffin Books, Penguin Random House Children's

80 Strand, London WC2R 0RL

The sun was low; the sultry air
Was almost more than he could bear.
A thunder roll foretold that strife
Would soon disturb this peaceful life.

Odysseus was lounging outside his palace on the island kingdom of Ithaca, enjoying the setting sun which was partly covered by a dark cloud. A sudden thought came to his mind: "The gods are jealous when man is too content." (And he *was* content indeed: with Penelope, his young wife,

Telemakhos, his baby son, and Argos, his puppy.) Life seemed too perfect and he felt a little nervous. At that very moment his herdsman ran up to say that a boat was approaching.

"Go down and meet the visitors!" said Odysseus. "I'll greet them here."

He soon learned the cause of their visit. Years ago he and all the other Greek kings had promised to come to King Menelaus's aid if ever he needed their help. The messengers were here to ask him to keep that promise. Menelaus's wife, Helen, had been captured by Paris, the Trojan king's son, and taken off to the city of Troy. Now Menelaus was gathering a force to attack Troy in order to bring her back.

So it was that Odysseus had to leave his perfect life. He quickly gathered a fleet of a dozen boats and set sail to join the other Greek kings on their way to Troy.

Odysseus hoped the battle would not last long and that he would soon return to Ithaca and his family. At Troy, he proved to be a fearsome fighter. Though not tall, he was strong as an ox, and his deep, mellow voice was the envy of all who met him.

But Zeus, the king of the gods, could not make up his mind to let the Greeks win, until his daughter, the goddess Athena, persuaded him that it was the Trojans who had caused the war by running off with Helen. The siege of Troy lasted for ten years. Only then did Zeus allow Odysseus to come up with a daring plan to defeat the Trojans.

"Let's pretend we have given up the struggle," Odysseus suggested one day to his fellow kings. "We'll strike camp and sail off as if we're going home but we'll leave the Trojans a present of a wooden horse. They won't suspect that soldiers will be hiding inside its belly. We'll build it so that you won't be able to see any sign that it's hollow; they'll take it into the city as a trophy and celebrate. Meanwhile our fleet will creep back and when the drunken Trojans have gone to sleep, our soldiers will remove the secret door in the horse's belly, climb out and open the gates to the rest of our army."

The plan was agreed. They built the horse, and the soldiers hid inside. Odysseus and the other kings destroyed their camp and sailed off. They left the wooden horse on the beach. When the Trojans found it, they were puzzled but then they began to laugh and to celebrate. Ten years of fighting were over! They dragged the horse into the city, and the feasting and the drinking began until they fell asleep, exhausted.

As planned, the Greek soldiers crept out and opened the gates. Their army poured into the city setting the houses alight with their burning torches.

King Menelaus charged up to the palace, where he found his wife. Odysseus was the hero of the Greek army. The fleets sailed away from Troy, and Odysseus felt proud of himself as he stood at the tiller of his boat. But Zeus, the king of the gods, watched as Odysseus puffed out his chest with pride and he determined to bring him down a peg or two. Zeus would make the journey home a nightmare for Odysseus.

Revenge is an attractive noun but kick your foe when he is down
And you may get a nasty fright, fortune changes overnight.

The first port that Odysseus and his fleet of boats stopped at was Ismarus. Because the people of Ismarus had supported Troy through the war, Odysseus destroyed the town and killed everyone except the priest, who gave him his best wine in gratitude. Odysseus wanted to leave without delay but his men insisted on having a feast. What a mistake! The locals from surrounding towns attacked them and many of Odysseus's men were killed before the rest could pull away in their ships. This was the first disaster Zeus brought upon Odysseus.

A gale sprang up and blew Odysseus's remaining fleet across the sea to the land of the lotus-eaters. Now anyone unwise enough to accept the lotus fruit, offered by the inhabitants, would fall immediately into a long, deep sleep, until all that was left of them would be a pile of bones. Odysseus sent some men inland to find food, warning them of the dangers. When they didn't return, he went after the men and found them lying under a tree, already dazed and half asleep. His men dragged them back to the boats and Odysseus ordered his fleet to pull away as fast as possible.

Because you find an open door, don't be tempted to explore.
But if you do find something tasty, hold hard! Don't be too hasty!

The next land they came to was on a beautiful part of the coast. No people were to be seen but sheep grazed in green pastures and trees gave welcome shade from the sun. Odysseus set off with his own crew to discover who lived here, leaving the other boats to wait for his return. Odysseus and his men took the delicious Ismarus wine with them.

They came across a cave with a smouldering fire, sheep in pens and cheese stacked on racks – it was a feast waiting for them! They killed a fat lamb, roasted it on the fire and finished off with a tasty cheese and a little wine.

It was only then that they heard someone approaching; a giant monster with a single eye entered the cave. The Cyclops came in followed by a herd of sheep. He closed the entrance with a rock that twenty humans could not have shifted. He sniffed the air, peered around the cave – and saw Odysseus and his men!

Odysseus greeted the Cyclops nervously. "The winds have driven our ship on to your shore. I trust you will welcome us as your guests." The Cyclops burst into laughter, grabbed two of the men and ate them for his supper. Then he lay down and went to sleep.

Odysseus was trapped. He knew that, even if he could kill the Cyclops, he and his men would never be able to shift the rock that blocked the entrance, so they spent the night at the back of the cave planning what to do.

The next morning the Cyclops grabbed two more men and ate them for his breakfast. Then he pushed aside the rock at the entrance, drove out his sheep and closed the gap again.

By the time the Cyclops returned in the evening and gobbled up two more of the crew, Odysseus was ready with his plan.

He offered the Cyclops a bowl of the Ismarus wine, which the giant swallowed in one gulp. The Cyclops had never tasted wine before. It was so delicious that he demanded more, immediately slurping it down.

Turning to Odysseus, he asked him what his name was.

Odysseus replied, "My name is Nobody."

"Then, Mr Nobody," said the Cyclops, "I'll do you a favour: I'll eat you last of all."

With that, he lay down and fell asleep. Odysseus and his men ran and fetched the trunk of an olive tree they had found at the back of the cave. They had already sharpened a point at one end. Now they made it red hot in the fire and drove it into the Cyclops's single eye.

The Cyclops screamed so loudly that other Cyclopes came to the entrance of his cave and called out, "What has happened to you, Polyphemus?"

"I have been blinded," he shouted.

"Who has done this?"

"Nobody has done it," he moaned in agony.

"What's all the fuss about then?" they answered, and returned to their caves, laughing.

When day broke, Polyphemus had to let his sheep out to graze. During the night Odysseus had tied each of his remaining men to the underbellies of three sheep. He himself clung on to the belly of the huge lead ram and left last of all. Luckily for Odysseus and his men, Polyphemus felt the backs of the sheep as they passed but not underneath them.

When the ram's turn came he said to him, "My dear old faithful friend, you always go out first. Is it because you know what has happened to me that today you leave last?"

And so with his clever plan Odysseus and his men escaped back to their ship. As their boat pulled out across the lagoon to re-join the rest of the fleet, Odysseus could not resist taunting Polyphemus who had chased after them, though his men begged their king to hold his tongue.

The furious giant scrambled to the water's edge and hurled a huge rock in the direction of the voice. It fell beyond them but made a wave so strong that

it drove the boat almost back to the shore. The oarsmen only just recovered in time to row swiftly away again but still Odysseus had to shout out:

"It was not Nobody but I, Odysseus, who gouged out your eye!"

In rage, Polyphemus called to his father Poseidon, god of the sea, to avenge him. Poseidon heard his anguished call and promised to put even more difficulties in the way of Odysseus's return.

The gods are not so very kind,
Annoy them and you'll find they mind.
You think you'll get a second chance?
You might be led a merry dance.

Next, Odysseus and his fleet came across the floating island of King Aeolus, to whom Zeus had given power over all the winds. King Aeolus welcomed Odysseus and his sailors, inviting them to join him and his family. They enjoyed a month of pleasure but Odysseus knew he and his men should continue to head for home. The king gave him the perfect present: a bag containing all the winds – well, all the winds except the gentle west wind that was left to blow Odysseus back home to Ithaca.

Odysseus knew he was the best helmsman so he took the tiller himself for seven days and seven nights. It was only when he saw the island of Ithaca in the distance and caught sight of the smoke rising from his palace that he handed over the tiller, lay down exhausted and dropped into a sound sleep.

Odysseus had never told his crew what was in the mysterious bag. Naturally they were curious: if it was wine, why should they not have a taste? Now at last was their chance to find out.

The moment the men untied the cord that secured the neck of the bag, out roared all the winds! The winds had only one aim: to return to their master, King Aeolus, as fast as possible. The boats were blown along at a terrifying pace and within a short time were all back at the floating island.

Odysseus made his way to the palace and explained to Aeolus what had happened but this time he got a very different reception. The king was furious: Odysseus had failed to look after his present. The king told him that he was not going to help someone whom the gods clearly despised.

"Take your leave immediately! Get out! Don't you dare come back again!" he shouted.

You have to hand it to Odysseus:
He alone remained suspicious.
Take care to look beyond the present!
The same truth holds for prince and peasant.

For seven days after they left King Aeolus, the fleet was driven by winds that were always blowing from the wrong direction. At last they came to an unknown shore. Here they found a harbour, protected by high cliffs, where Odysseus's sailors insisted on anchoring. Odysseus himself feared that if there was trouble a quick getaway might be difficult so he moored his boat outside the harbour.

Three of the crew set off to discover who lived in this place and came across a giant who said she was the daughter of the king and that her people were the Laestrygonians.

She offered to take them to her father's palace but when they met the king, an even larger and more terrifying giant, he grabbed one of the men and ate him on the spot. The other two ran back to warn the fleet to leave with all possible haste but they were pursued by the giants, who stood on the cliffs and rained down rocks. The boats were all destroyed and the crews killed and eaten. Only Odysseus with his one boat and crew, moored outside the harbour, was able to escape.

Zeus had struck again.

Odysseus sailed on until he reached another island. He sent out a party that came across a pack of wolves. They did not know that these creatures had once been men but had been turned into wild animals by the enchantress Circe. When they reached a house, Circe herself came out to meet them. She invited them in; only one man, Eurylochos, suspected a trap and stayed outside. The others followed her and were given food and wine, but the wine contained a drug that turned them into swine. Circe herded them into a pigsty.

Eurylochos ran back to tell Odysseus who set out at once to rescue his crew.

On the way he met the god Hermes, sent by Athena to help him. Hermes gave him a magic plant to give him protection against Circe's spells.

When Circe met him, she offered Odysseus wine. He gulped it down, then drew his sword and raised it to strike her. She had been warned that one day a stranger would arrive and not be affected by her magic potion, so she invited Odysseus into her home. He lowered his sword and said he would follow her when she had promised to release his crew. Circe opened the pigsty and made a spell. The pigs shed their bristles, stopped grunting, stood up and became human again.

The crew lived in Circe's home for a whole year. But Odysseus longed to go home and at last Circe agreed to let him. She told him that before he headed back to Ithaca he must descend to the Underworld in order to get advice from the ghost of Teiresias, a prophet who could see into the future.

The men were not keen to go to such a frightening place but Odysseus convinced them that there was no choice.

Odysseus and his crew were blown by the north wind to the end of the known world. They sailed along the coast until they found the entrance to Hades, a place where two rivers met. The waters seethed and churned, giving off a terrible stench, but Odysseus and his men passed through the entrance until they reached a barren shore. They followed Circe's instructions: they dug a trench and poured in milk and honey, wine and water. Finally they sacrificed a ram and a black ewe that she had given them and let the blood pour into the trench.

Circe had told Odysseus not to let anyone, however eager they were, drink the blood before the ghost of Teiresias had drunk his fill. Only this would give him the strength to speak. When Teiresias appeared out of the swirling mist, he went straight to the trench and without a word gulped down the strange mixture.

Then in a solemn voice he told Odysseus that Poseidon was so angry that he would make Odysseus's journey home a nightmare. He said that he would eventually reach Ithaca, as long as he or his men did not kill the cattle of Helios, the sun-god. Finally he added:

"Be warned! Young noblemen have invaded your palace and are wooing your wife, Penelope."

When Odysseus's mother's ghost appeared, it was a terrible shock: he had no idea that she had died while he was away at war. She sipped the mixture before looking up at him and telling him that grief had killed her after he had left. Three times he tried to embrace his mother but each time her ghost melted away and slipped through his arms.

Odysseus could bear no more. He and his crew continued on their way.

When people promise you the moon
A smart "goodbye!" can't come too soon.

Back at sea, the land of the Sirens came into view. Circe had warned Odysseus about these weird creatures who had the faces of beautiful girls and such enchanting voices that once you heard them you were lost. The Sirens lived by the sea in fields littered with the bones of sailors they had lured to their death.

Odysseus gave orders: "Plug your ears with wax and tie me to the mast as we approach the home of the Sirens! Row past as fast as you can and do not release me, even if I beg you to!"

When the Sirens surrounded the ship, sang their songs and promised to tell Odysseus about what the future held in store for him, he shouted, "Untie me, untie me, I say!" But the sailors bound him even more tightly to the mast until they were well past the cursed spot.

Worse difficulties lay ahead. The ships had to go through a narrow sea channel: on one side was a monster whirlpool, Charybdis – if they sailed too close they would be sucked down and spat out dead. Circe had warned them about this too, but there was a danger on the other side of the channel that they had forgotten about: an evil monster called Scylla who had six long necks. Each neck ended in a mouth packed with razor-sharp teeth. While Odysseus's crew were gazing into the abyss of the whirlpool, Scylla struck. Within seconds each mouth held a struggling sailor and lifted them up the cliff face to the cave where Scylla lived. The rest of the crew watched in horror as the monster devoured their mates with blood-curdling yelping sounds.

When you're told to "shut that door!"
And that instruction you ignore,
Things can take a nasty turn.
Sometimes it's too late to learn.

Exhausted, Odysseus and his crew beached their boat on the island that was the home of the sun-god Helios's cattle, which they had been warned not to kill. But the wind made it impossible to sail further. Their food ran out – and their hunger pangs became unbearable.

One day, while Odysseus was absent, Eurylochos said to his shipmates, "Let's kill a couple of calves. When we reach Ithaca, we'll build a temple to Helios to make up for killing his precious cattle. I'm sure he won't mind."

But Helios did mind. When he found that Odysseus's crew had killed his cattle, he asked Zeus to punish them. And Zeus agreed.

Finally the winds changed and, although the boat was able to put to sea, Zeus sent a raging storm. The boat sank with the loss of all the crew except Odysseus. He was thrown overboard and only survived by clinging to some flotsam.

Odysseus was now alone in a rough sea. Clinging to a spar, he was driven by the winds for nine days until, half dead with exhaustion, he washed up on the island home of the goddess Calypso.

Calypso fell in love with Odysseus at first sight and offered him a perfect life if only he would stay with her.

Well, he stayed for seven years, doing whatever she wanted, but he never for a moment forgot his wife and son. He often sat by the shore, weeping. Finally the goddess Athena could endure it no longer: she convinced her father, Zeus, that Odysseus had suffered enough.

Zeus sent his messenger to tell Calypso she must release Odysseus. She

agreed and gave him the materials and tools to build himself a sturdy raft. He launched it into the sea and, dressed in the fine clothes she had given him, kissed the tearful goddess goodbye and set sail in a gentle breeze.

Poseidon caught sight of Odysseus on his raft, heading for Ithaca. He had still not forgiven him for blinding his son Polyphemus, so, without telling Zeus, he sent a howling gale that swept Odysseus off his raft. Odysseus was dragged down in the sea and only when his lungs were near to bursting did he manage to free himself and swim to the surface. When he had scrambled back on to the raft, a goddess disguised as a bird gave him a length of magic cloth to tie round his waist. Poseidon sent an even larger wave that wrecked the raft altogether but Odysseus was kept afloat by the cloth.

By this time Poseidon had returned to his home in the depths of the sea, so Athena sent a wind to flatten the waves. Odysseus swam for seven days and seven nights until he reached an island. By the time he had scrambled ashore, his legs and body were raw with wounds. He dragged himself up the beach and fell into a deep sleep under some bushes.

The next morning he was woken by the cheerful sound of girls' voices. When he emerged from the bushes, all the girls ran away in terror, except one, Nausikaa, daughter of King Alcinous. Odysseus looked a bit like a dishevelled lion, but he soon charmed Nausikaa, who gave him food, drink and clothes. She had come down to the shore with her servants to do the family washing and when it had dried she loaded her cart and took him to meet her parents.

The king and queen lived in a beautiful palace with bronze walls, silver pillars and golden doors, guarded by silver watchdogs. They welcomed the shipwrecked stranger and prepared a luxurious feast to entertain him.

During the feast a blind bard, Demodicus, sang to the guests the story of the Trojan War and the wooden horse. Odysseus could not help crying openly as he listened to the account of his own adventures. He told them he was the hero of the song. By this time Nausikaa had fallen in love with him, but when he said how he longed to return to his wife and son, and how he had already been away for twenty years, King Alcinous promised to help him.

One of the king's fastest boats, with twenty of his best oarsmen, was loaded with gifts; Odysseus went aboard and fell fast asleep while the crew rowed him in record time to Ithaca. He had not yet woken up when they reached the island, so they laid him down by the shore and piled all the gifts nearby. He was home at last.

You've been away for twenty years?
On your return expect some tears.
The boy's grown up, the dog is dying.
Your pleasure will be tinged with sighing.

Odysseus woke up to find a landscape that he did not recognize. Then it was that Athena approached him.

She told him how sorry she was for taking so long to help him get back to Ithaca. She warned him that noblemen from all over his kingdom had been courting his wife. For the last three years they had slept in his palace whenever it suited them and killed his cattle for their feasts. Odysseus knew he must avenge these wrongs. Athena disguised him as an old beggar, then she sent him off to the cottage where Eumaius, the faithful swineherd, lived.

Because of the clever disguise, Eumaius did not recognize his dear master when he met him and believed his tale of being someone who bore news of Odysseus. He invited the poor man into his home and gave him a meal.

The next morning Eumaius had left for work when Odysseus's son, Telemakhos, came to the door. Telemakhos, now a fine young man, had been away on a voyage to ask King Menelaus if he had any news of his father's whereabouts. At this moment Athena temporarily lifted Odysseus's disguise, revealing his true self.

He turned to his son and said, "Telemakhos, my son, my son, I am your father! I have returned at last." They hugged each other and wept for all the lost years.

At last they could plot their revenge. Athena restored Odysseus's disguise before Eumaius returned and then they all set out for the palace.

At the entrance Odysseus spotted an old hunting dog lying on a dung heap. He knew it was Argos, and Argos knew his old master. The dog raised his head, drooped his tattered ears, wagged his tail, let out a little yelp and then dropped down dead.

Inside the palace, the suitors were feasting when Odysseus, dressed in his rags, walked in. As the custom required, they all offered him food, except for Antinous who threw a stool at him.

Penelope heard that Antinous had treated a beggar rudely and invited the beggar up to her rooms. She warmed to him and she even confided in him how she had put off the suitors for the last three years. She said she would only marry when she had finished weaving a shroud for her old father-in-law who might die soon. Each night she unpicked the work she had done during the day, but the suitors had recently discovered this. She could put them off no longer.

She told him how she planned to marry the man who could string her husband's great bow and shoot an arrow through the rings of a dozen double-headed axes. Odysseus had amazed her with this feat when he was a young man.

Odysseus did not reveal his true identity, but the old nurse, who was told to bathe his feet, recognized a scar on his leg and knew him. Before she could cry out, he stopped her mouth with his hand and said, "Keep it to yourself a little longer!"

The next day the suitors arrived for another feast. Penelope brought out the great bow and each man tried in turn to string it; they all failed. Meanwhile Odysseus had slipped away to tell Eumaius who he really was.

"Collect all the swords and spears you can find and take them to the cellar!" he ordered.

When Odysseus returned to the hall, Penelope insisted the beggar be given a chance to string the bow. Telemakhos knew the fighting would start soon and ordered his mother to go up to her rooms. Odysseus strung the bow with ease and then shot an arrow cleanly through the twelve axe rings. The next arrow was aimed at Antinous and found its mark: Antinous fell dead.

The suitors ran to get their swords and spears, but the weapons were gone – taken to the cellar by Eumaius. Odysseus, his son and his cowherd were pitted against all the suitors but only they were armed and they had the help of the goddess Athena. It was not long before all the suitors were dead.

Only now was Penelope told what the uproar was all about. Odysseus bathed and dressed in fine clothes before going to her rooms, but she was slow to recognize her husband. However, when he described the marriage bed that he himself had made, she no longer held back, for that was a secret known only to the two of them. At last she believed her eyes and held him to her as if she would never let him go.

*Our story's
done, the die is cast.
Our hero has come home at last.
The wicked paid a dreadful price.
Did you think all gods were nice?
None of his gallant crew is left
And all their wives are now bereft.
Not to mention lasses and lads
Or sad, despairing mums and dads.
Heroes achieve great deeds of fame.
They leave behind the dead
and lame.*

How to say the names in *The Odyssey*

Name	How to say it
Aeolus	Ee-*oh*-lus
Alcinous	Al-kin-*o*-us
Antinous	An-*ti*-no-us
Argos	*Ar*-gos
Athena	Ath-*ee*-na
Calypso	Ka-*lip*-so
Charybdis	Kar-*ib*-dis
Circe	*Sir*-see
Cyclops	*Sy*-klops
Demodicus	De-*mod*-i-kus
Eumaius	You-*may*-us
Eurylochos	You-*ril*-o-kus
Hades	*Hay*-dees
Helios	*Hee*-li-os
Hermes	*Her*-meez
Ismarus	*Iz*-mar-us
Ithaca	*Ith*-a-ka
Laestrygonians	Lie-stri-*go*-nians
Menelaus	Men-e-*lay*-us
Nausikaa	*Nor*-si-*kay*-a
Odysseus	O-*di*-si-us
Polyphemus	Po-li-*fee*-mus
Poseidon	Pos-*eye*-den
Scylla	Skil-uh
Sirens	*Sigh*-rens
Teiresias	Ty-*ree*-si-us
Telemakhos	Tel-*em*-ak-us
Zeus	Ze-youss